THE USBORNE BOOK OF POP-UPS

Ray Gibson and Louisa Somerville

Designed by Carol Law

Illustrated by Angie Sage

Contents

First published in 1990. This edition 1992. Usborne Publishing Ltd, Usborne House, 83-85 Saffron Hill, London EC1N 8RT, England. Copyright © 1992, 1990. Usborne Publishing Ltd.

The name Usborne and the device are Trade Marks of Usborne Publishing Ltd. All rights reserved.

Getting started

In this book you can find out how to make all sorts of pop-up cards and other pop-up projects. Step-by-step pictures show you how to make them. Most are quite simple. Make them just for fun, or give them to people on special occasions. Here are some tips to help you before you start.

Things you will need

To make the cards you need these things, plus a few extras, such as paperclips.

Thin card in lots of colours

Thin white paper, such as typing paper

Scissors

Pencil and ruler

Felt tip pens

Powder and poster paints

Paint brushes

Stick of glue

Coloured inks

Measuring

To make each card in this book, you will need to cut and fold a rectangle of card or paper.

Measurements are given at the top of the page.

All measurements are for cards before they are folded.

10cm (4in)

16cm (6½in)

Before you start each card, turn to the page to see what size rectangle you need to cut.

If it says 10 x 16cm (4 x 6½in), you must cut a card 10cm(4in) wide and 16cm(6½in) long.

Cutting

Here's how to make sure you cut the edges of the card straight.

Measure from the left-hand edge of the paper, near the top. Make a dot at the right number of centimetres (inches).

Further down the card, measure and mark again.

Draw a line down the card, through the dots. Cut along it to make a straight edge.

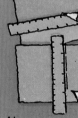

Always use a ruler to draw straight lines.

Folding

In this book, two sorts of fold are used a lot.

A mountain fold looks like this.

A valley fold looks like this.

Always fold the longer sides in half.

When you fold a card, press the middle first. Smooth it down with your fingers. Then press outwards from side to side.

Make all folds neatly and press them firmly with your finger and thumb or with a ruler.

Lines you fold are shown like this.

Lines you cut are shown like this.

Decoration

Collect all kinds of bits and bobs to brighten up your pop-ups. These things would be useful.

Pictures cut from magazines

Sequins

Glitter

Scraps of ribbon and lace

Feathers

Wallpaper and wrapping paper

Gold and silver foil

Gold and silver pens (for writing on coloured card)

Finishing touches

Add a picture or a message to the front of the card. Remember to sign it inside, too.

Happy birthday

Congratulations

Be my honey bear

Growl!

Love Billy x

Get well soon

Simple pop-ups

Stand-up card

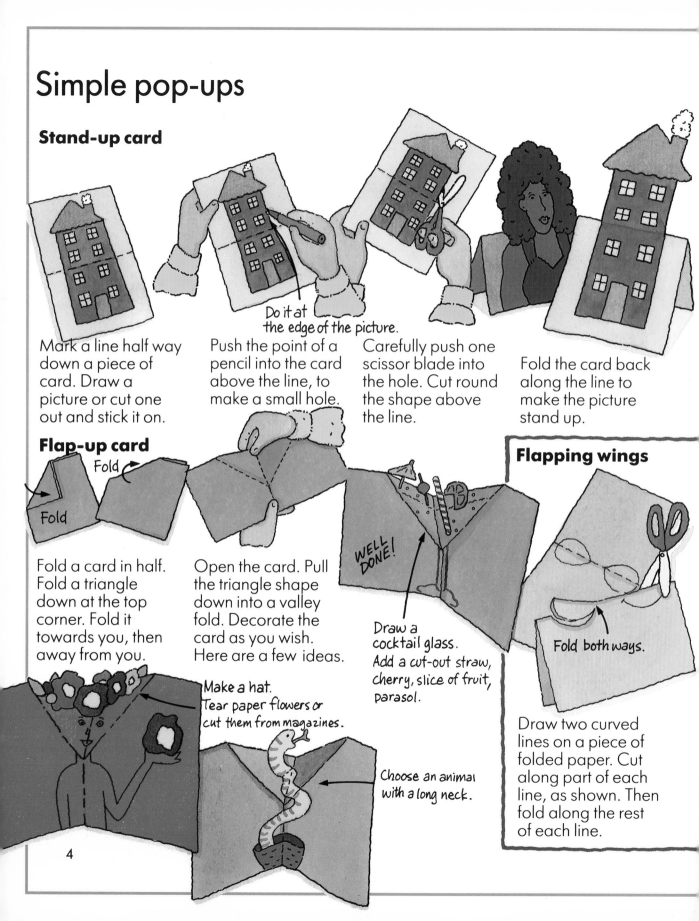

Do it at the edge of the picture.

Mark a line half way down a piece of card. Draw a picture or cut one out and stick it on.

Push the point of a pencil into the card above the line, to make a small hole.

Carefully push one scissor blade into the hole. Cut round the shape above the line.

Fold the card back along the line to make the picture stand up.

Flap-up card

Fold

Fold

Fold a card in half. Fold a triangle down at the top corner. Fold it towards you, then away from you.

Open the card. Pull the triangle shape down into a valley fold. Decorate the card as you wish. Here are a few ideas.

WELL DONE!

Draw a cocktail glass. Add a cut-out straw, cherry, slice of fruit, parasol.

Make a hat. Tear paper flowers or cut them from magazines.

Choose an animal with a long neck.

Flapping wings

Fold both ways.

Draw two curved lines on a piece of folded paper. Cut along part of each line, as shown. Then fold along the rest of each line.

4

Genie in a jar

You will need an empty plastic jar with a screw-on lid. Mix poster paint and glue and paint inside the jar.

This is called an accordion fold.

Cut a strip of card three times the height of the jar. Make narrow folds along it (as you would for a fan).

Cut out and colour a genie. Glue it to the top of the folded strip. Stick a feather and some strong thread to the genie's turban.

When you take off the lid, the genie will pop out.

Glue the bottom of the folded strip inside the jar. Tape the end of the thread to the jar lid and screw it on.

BEE HAPPY!

Open the paper and pull the "wings" towards you. Stick the paper onto a card the same size.

Draw a bee's body between the wings. Open and close the card to make the bee's wings flap.

Another idea

Make a single flap as shown, for a newspaper or book.

More ideas

Accordion fold a strip of paper. Glue the ends inside a folded card. The folded strip can be a ballerina's skirt or a clown's ruff.

Pig with stand-out snout

Fold a piece of pink or white card, about 30 x 15cm (12 x 6in). Put it on one side while you make a spring.

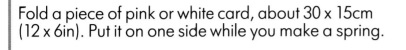

To make a spring

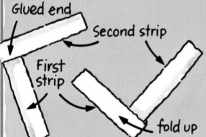

Cut two paper strips, each 1.5 x 15cm(½ x 6in). Dab glue at the end of the first.

Glued end
Second strip
First strip
fold up

Press the second strip on to the glued end at right-angles. Fold the first strip up over the second strip. Carry on folding the strips across each other, until all the paper is used up.

Dab some glue under the top flap and press down. Cut off any extra paper to leave a folded square shape.

Cut   Glue

Inside the card

Rub out the lines in the middle of the ears

Draw a pair of feet

Don't use anything to draw round. A wobbly shape is nicer.

Draw a large circle in pencil on the right-hand side, nearer the top than the bottom. Add two ears.

Go over the lines with black felt tip. Glue one end of the spring and press it into the middle of the circle.

To make the snout

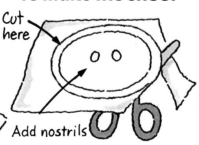

Cut here

Add nostrils

On a piece of card draw a circle in black felt tip. It must be big enough to cover the spring. Cut around the circle outside the line.

Tip

You could give your pig a flower to carry. Make one out of card or cut one from a magazine. Glue the flower between the spring and the snout.

To finish the card

Glue the snout to the top of the spring. The snout will stand out when you open the card.

Draw in the eyes

ON YOUR BIRTHDAY...

MAKE A PIG OF YOURSELF!

Add texture

Dab your pig with a sponge dipped in thick pink paint to give it a mottled look.

Print some straw by dabbing the card with a piece of drinking straw dipped in yellow paint.

Other ideas

Snake pit

For the snakes' bodies, make three springs of different sizes out of wrapping paper or wallpaper.

Valley fold

Add eyes, nostrils and a tongue

Cut a head for each snake. Make a valley fold near the end of each head. Glue the heads to the bodies.

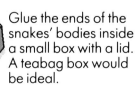

Glue the ends of the snakes' bodies inside a small box with a lid. A teabag box would be ideal.

Glue the back of each head to the box lid. Close the box. When you open it the snakes will rear up.

Boxer

Glue a spring behind the boxing glove

7

Dancing snowmen

The arms must touch the sides of the paper.

This is an accordion fold.

Fold a piece of white paper, 13 x 30cm(5 x 12in). Fold each side outwards in half again. The edges must line up with the centre fold.

Keeping the paper folded, lightly draw a circle for a snowman's head. Draw an oval for the body. Then add arms, legs and a hat.

Go over the outline with a pencil crayon. Rub out all the other pencil lines.

Fix the snowmen

Fold a piece of black card, 16 x 30cm(6½ x 12in). Put some glue on the backs of the first and last snowmen.

Lay the middle fold of the snowmen along the centre fold of the card. Lay them nearer the top than the bottom of the card.

Press the snowmen down. Pull the two in the middle towards you and close the card. When you open the card, they will stand out.

You could draw stars in pencil on the snowman to remind yourself where not to cut.

Make sure the pencil outlines are on the back.

Cut around the outline. Keep the paper folded. Be careful not to cut around the ends of the snowman's arms.

Carefully open out the snowmen. Add faces, scarves and so on. You could make each one different.

Add a snowy lawn

Paint some falling snow

Snip here

Cut a strip of white paper, 4 x 30cm(1½ x 12in). Fold it in the same way as for the snowmen. Snip bumpy shapes in the top.

Glue the lawn to the card in the same way as you glued the snowmen. Leave a space between the snowmen and the lawn.

Other ideas

Draw different Christmas pictures. Each shape must touch the sides of the folded paper.

Christmas trees and stars

Crackers

MERRY   CHRISTMAS

You could make cards like these for other occasions, such as birthdays.

Birthday cakes

Happy   Birthday

Dancing frogs

Floating ghost

Cut two pieces of black card 11 x 19cm(4½ x 7½in). Fold them in half and put one aside.

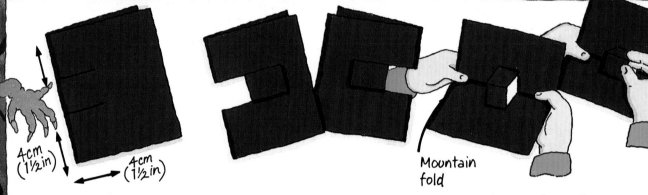

4cm (1½in)

4cm (1½in)

Mountain fold

Make two marks on the folded edge, 4cm(1½in) from each end. Draw two 4cm(1½in) lines from the marks. Cut along them.

Fold the cut middle piece back and press down. Open the flap. Turn the card over and repeat the fold. Open out the flap.

Open the card out. Press the middle piece up from behind into a box shape. Pinch up and crease the centre fold of the box.

Add ghostly noises in silver pen or white paint.

You could stick on a picture cut from a magazine instead.

Cut roughly around the ghost. Then carefully cut it out, leaving a black edge. Turn the ghost over and put some glue near the bottom.

Stick the ghost to the front of the box. It will look as if it is floating against the blackness.

If you make the box smaller, you will have room for a taller ghost.

The box is folded inside the card.

Line up the edge of the paper with the edge of the box.

Close the card and press it. Open the card again and turn it over. Spread glue around the edges of the card.

Lay the card over the second card, matching the centre folds. Press them together. Then gently pull the box towards you.

Put some white paper in front of the box. With black felt-tip, draw a ghost shape inside the area shown by a dotted line.

Other ideas
Spaceman

Add floating things stuck on springs (see page 6).

Cut a flap and draw a picture underneath.

Diving woman
Make the card wider, 15cm(6in) for example. Cut two boxes.

Diver on spring

First draw some legs on the box. Then draw the rest of the body on the card.

Shark and seagull on boxes

ENJOY YOUR HOLIDAY!

Tip
This is a way to make a box of a different colour to the card.

Tab

Cut a strip of card with tabs as shown.

Tab

Fold the tabs under and glue the strip to a card, matching the centre folds.

Centre folds

11

Gobbling monster

Fold a piece of red card and one of white paper, each 20 x 28cm(8 x 11in). Put the card aside.

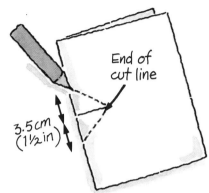

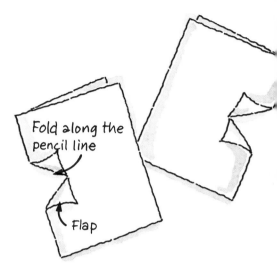

End of cut line

Fold along the pencil line

Flap

To make the mouth

Mark the folded edge of the paper 10cm(4in) from the end. Draw a 5cm(2in) line from the mark and cut along it.

Make a mark each side of the cut line, 3.5cm(1½in) away from it. Draw a line from each mark to the end of the cut line.

Fold back two flaps. Open out the flaps and turn the paper over. Fold the flaps down and then open them out again.

When you open and close the card, the triangles will flap open and shut, like a mouth.

Lay the paper out flat. Pinch up the folds at each end of the paper. They will change from valley folds to mountain folds.

As you pinch them up, push the folded triangle shapes through to the other side. Press the card to flatten the triangles inside.

Open the red card and put glue on the outside edges only. Lay the white paper on top, matching the centre folds.

Inside the card

Draw a monster around the mouth and colour it. You could make smudgy prints all over it with a small piece of sponge dipped in ink or paint.

COME TO MY PARTY... THERE'LL BE LOTS TO EAT

Legs to gobble

4cm (1½ in)

1cm (½ in)

Draw a line on paper 1cm(½in) from the top. Mark two 4cm(1½in) widths to make tabs and draw some legs below. Cut around the legs and tabs.

Stick on sequins, stars or glitter if you like.

Colour in the legs on both sides. Glue under the tabs and stick them inside the monster's lower jaw so that the legs hang out.

Tip

If you make several invitation cards, accordion fold the paper first. Then you can cut lots of legs out at one time.

Other ideas

Make a jagged cut in the folded paper to look like some teeth.

Stick a 'victim' inside

Add a tongue

Jagged cut

Cut two slits in the folded paper. Rotate the card so that the slits are side by side. Now they can be a cat's eyes or car headlights.

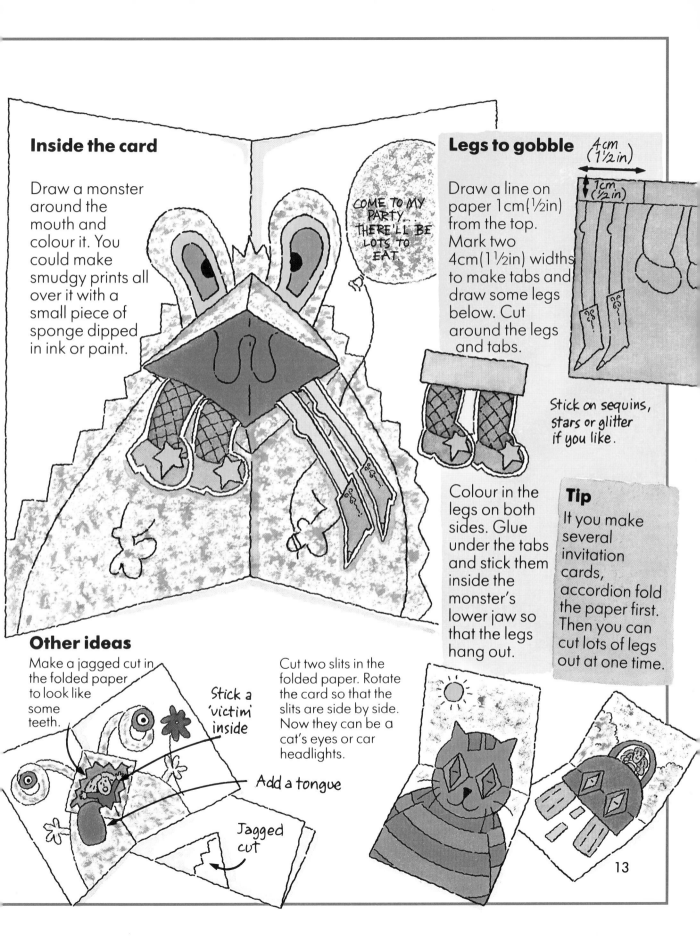

Inkblot demon

This makes your demon.

You could add more colours and fold again.

Cut outside the demon's edge.

Cut from the bottom edge of the paper.

1.5cm (¾in)

Drip a few drops of ink or runny paint into the centre of a folded piece of stiff white paper, 13 x 17cm(5 x 6½in).

Close the paper carefully. Press it, to spread the ink out. Open the card and leave it to dry.

Crease the fold the other way, so it changes from a valley fold into a mountain fold. Cut around the demon.

Draw a line across 1.5cm(¾in) from the bottom. Snip the corner off to where the line meets the centre fold.

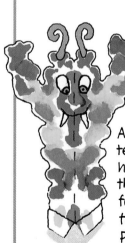

Add eyes, teeth or horns. Cut them from folded paper, to make pairs.

To make the card

5.5cm (2¼in)

Open the demon out and mountain fold along the lines, to make two tabs. Add eyes, fangs and horns if you like.

Fold a card, 18 x 25cm(7 x 10in). Put a pencil dot on the fold 5.5cms(2¼in) from the top. Draw lines from the dot to the top corners.

Glue the tabs. Put the demon on the pencil dot with the tabs folded behind. Line up each tab along a pencil line and press.

When the glue is dry, fold and press the card. The demon will rear up when you open it again.

Add some scenery

Make more inkblots for scenery in front of your demon. Trim them to look like flames, a jungle or a city skyline.

In front of the demon, mark a dot on the fold for the next pop-up. Measure the distance from the dot to the demon.

Measure and mark the same distance from the top corners down each side of the card. Draw lines from the centre dot to the dots on the edges.

Measure the scenery to make sure it will fit in the space. You may need to trim it a bit. Make tabs along the bottom, as before.

Glue here

Glue the tabs along the pencil lines.

Other ideas

Cut the inkblot into a butterfly shape. Stick it on a box (see page 10) or spring (see page 6).

Make a tiny monster. Drip a small blob of paint or ink on paper. Spread it outwards using a straw or the blunt end of a paintbrush.

When it is dry, stick on cut-out eyes, feet and so on. Mount it on a box or spring.

Tip

To make long, low scenery, smooth the paint from the fold towards the paper's edge.

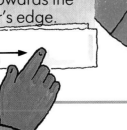

15

Bat and moon

Trace the bat template on page 32 onto a folded black card, 12 x 24cm (4½ x 9in).

Remember to trace the fold line on the wing.

Trace the bat template on page 32

Tip

If the pencil line does not show up well enough, go over it with a white or yellow pencil crayon.

Do not trace over this line.

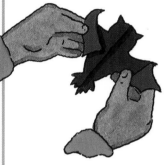

Cut the bat out. Fold the wings along the fold lines, first one way, then the other.

Open out the bat, so the centre fold is a mountain fold. Make valley folds on both wings.

Turn the bat over. Put glue between the wing-tips and the wing folds. Turn it over again.

Stick the bat inside a blue card, 15 x 25cm(6 x 10in). Match centre folds. Leave it to dry.

Cut out a big round or crescent moon. Glue it on the card so that the bat stands out in front of it.

Other ideas

Add a church, a tree or some stars to the background.

Try out different colours for the sky and moon.

Close the card gently, pulling the centre fold of the bat towards you. Press all over the card.

16

Rocket

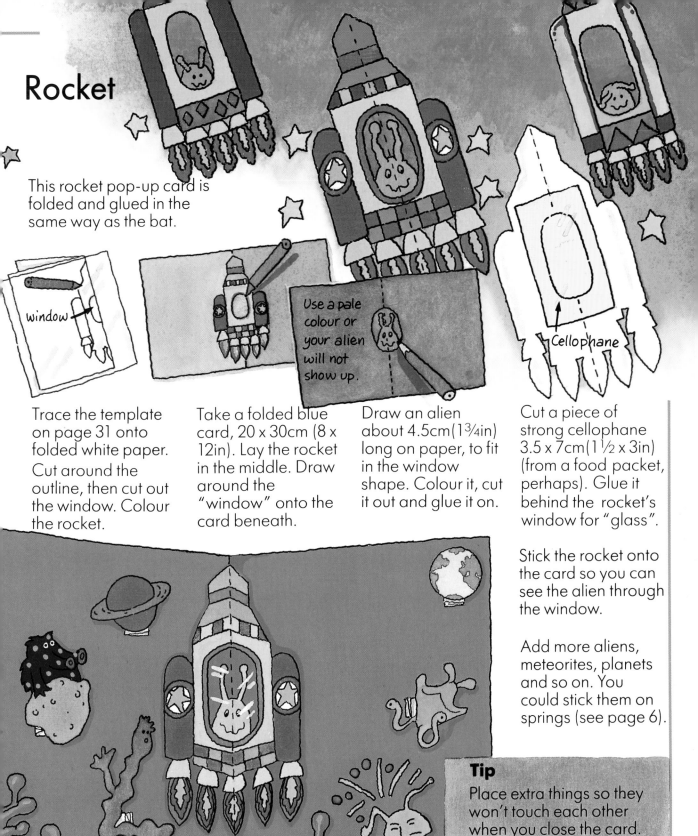

This rocket pop-up card is folded and glued in the same way as the bat.

window

Use a pale colour or your alien will not show up.

Cellophane

Trace the template on page 31 onto folded white paper. Cut around the outline, then cut out the window. Colour the rocket.

Take a folded blue card, 20 x 30cm (8 x 12in). Lay the rocket in the middle. Draw around the "window" onto the card beneath.

Draw an alien about 4.5cm(1¾in) long on paper, to fit in the window shape. Colour it, cut it out and glue it on.

Cut a piece of strong cellophane 3.5 x 7cm(1½ x 3in) (from a food packet, perhaps). Glue it behind the rocket's window for "glass".

Stick the rocket onto the card so you can see the alien through the window.

Add more aliens, meteorites, planets and so on. You could stick them on springs (see page 6).

Tip
Place extra things so they won't touch each other when you close the card.

17

Cancan pigs

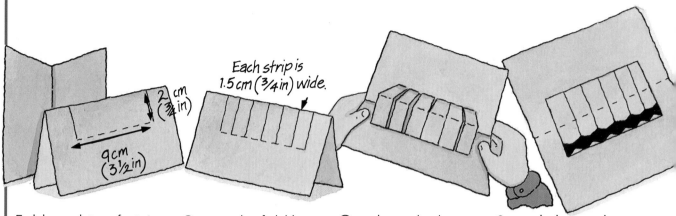

Each strip is 1.5cm (¾in) wide.

2cm (¾in)

9cm (3½in)

Fold two bits of pink card, 15 x 16cm (6 x 6½in). On one card draw and cut a box shape (see page 10).

Crease the fold line but do not push the box through. Mark off the box into six equal strips for legs.

Cut along the lines. Open the card and push the box shape through.

Smooth the card out flat. Draw and colour a foot at the end of each leg.

Inside the card

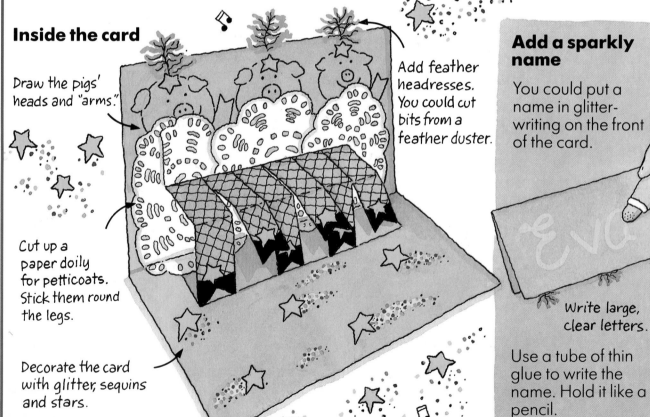

Draw the pigs' heads and "arms."

Add feather headresses. You could cut bits from a feather duster.

Cut up a paper doily for petticoats. Stick them round the legs.

Decorate the card with glitter, sequins and stars.

Add a sparkly name

You could put a name in glitter-writing on the front of the card.

Write large, clear letters.

Use a tube of thin glue to write the name. Hold it like a pencil.

Draw criss-cross lines in black felt tip on each leg to look like fishnet tights.

Snip across the base of legs 2, 4 and 6 so they can "kick". Trim the ends of the feet.

Turn the card over. Draw fishnets and a foot on the back of each kicking leg.

Turn the card over again and glue it to the second card. Bend the legs to make them kick.

Sprinkle glitter all over the card and tip it off again. Some glitter will stick to the writing, so it sparkles.

Add sequins and stars, if you like.

Tip

When you tip the glitter off, put some folded paper underneath. The fold in the paper will make it easier to pour the glitter back into the tube.

Other ideas

Dancers

Draw different sorts of dancers. You could give them legs that don't match.

Draw in the shoes.

Dracula

If you turn the card around, the strips can be Dracula's fingers.

Make these cuts at a slant, to shape the hands.

Cut four strips, for fingers.

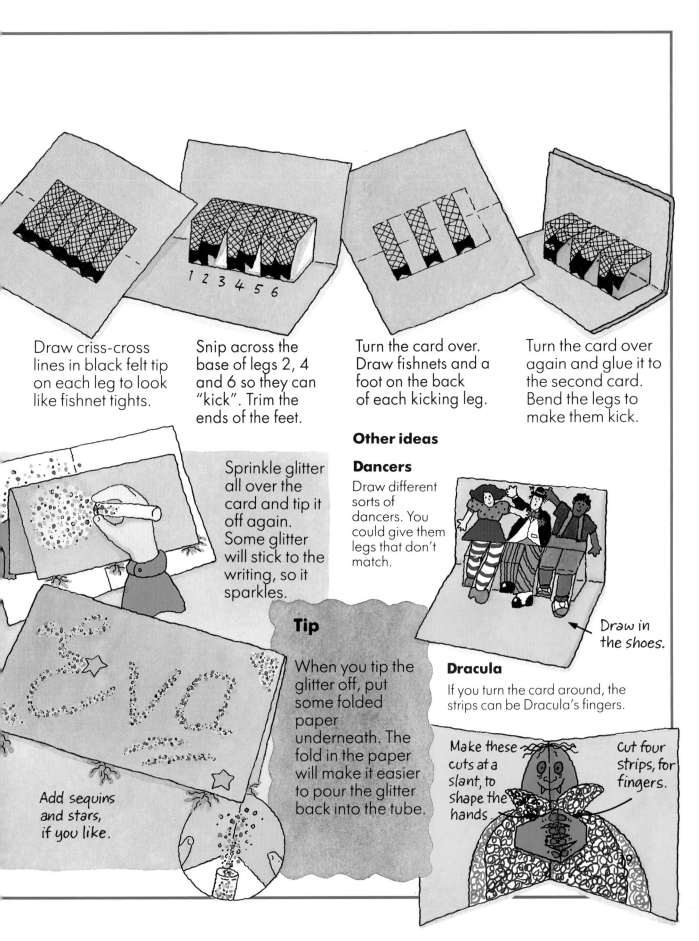

Curse of the mummy's tomb

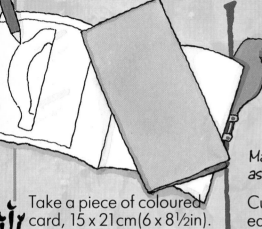

Take a piece of coloured card, 15 x 21cm (6 x 8½in). Fold it in half lengthways to make a tall, thin card. Trace the mummy's tomb template on page 32.

Make the strips as thin as you can.

Cut strips from the folded edge straight across towards the middle. End each cut at the outline of the mummy.

Outline of mummy

Make sure all the strips go through to the other side.

Unfold the strips again and smooth them flat. Very carefully open the paper out flat. Pinch up the ends and press the strips through to the other side.

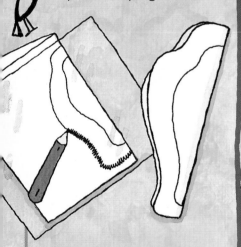

Fold a piece of white paper. Trace the shape onto the paper. Go over the lines with black felt tip. Then cut around the shape.

Tip

If you are worried about cutting straight, draw the lines first with a pencil and ruler.

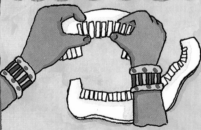

Fold the strips back along the outline. Fold a few at a time, starting with the ones in the middle. Unfold the strips. Turn the paper over and fold them again.

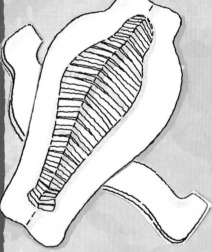

Fold the paper and press the strips flat. Open the paper out to see the mummy wrapped in bandages.

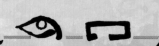
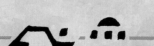

To decorate the mummy

Draw a line 0.5cm(¼in) from the edge all the way around, as a margin. Colour the margin brown, for the mummy's wooden tomb (called the sarcophagus).

Use dark paint to fill in between the margin and the mummy, to make it look dark inside the sarcophagus.

Draw hieroglyphics (Egyptian picture symbols) inside the sarcophagus. Look in books about Ancient Egypt for ideas.

To finish the card

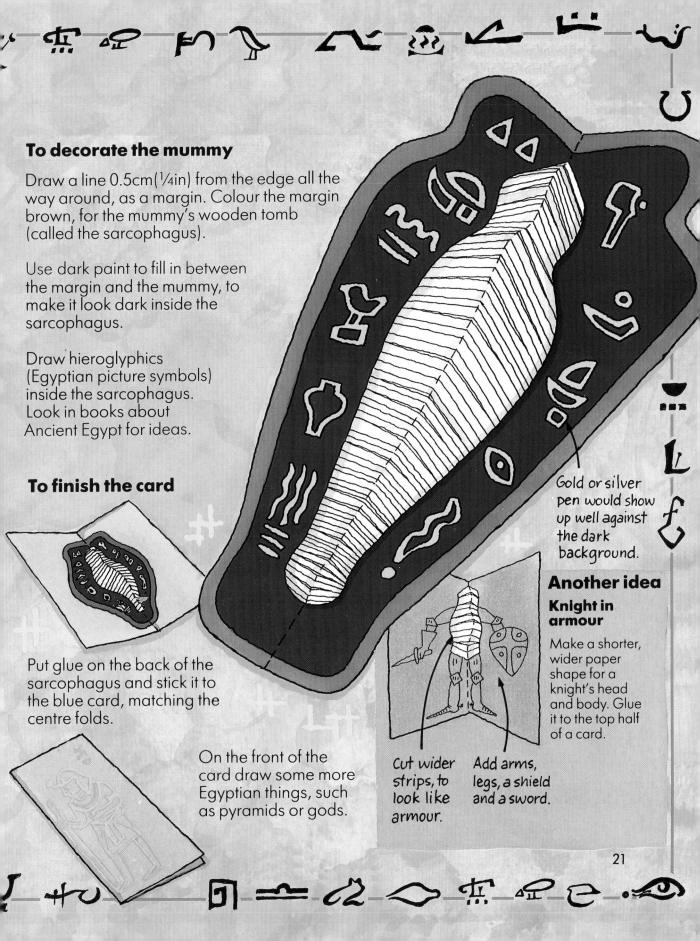

Gold or silver pen would show up well against the dark background.

Put glue on the back of the sarcophagus and stick it to the blue card, matching the centre folds.

On the front of the card draw some more Egyptian things, such as pyramids or gods.

Another idea
Knight in armour

Make a shorter, wider paper shape for a knight's head and body. Glue it to the top half of a card.

Cut wider strips, to look like armour.

Add arms, legs, a shield and a sword.

Sickly beast

Fold two pieces of white or pale-coloured paper, 15 x 28cm(6 x 11in).

Make a pair of beast's eyes

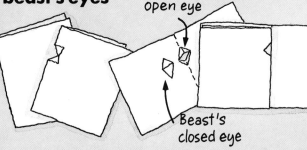

Beast's open eye

Beast's closed eye

Mark 5cm(2in) down the folded edge of one card. Make a 1.5cm(½in) cut. Fold back two flaps. Then fold them inside the card (see page 12).

Next to the "eye", draw a matching diamond shape to look like a closed eye. Close the card and put it on top of the other open card.

Draw along the edges of the V shape to make a V on the lower card. Then draw another V so it now makes a diamond.

Lift off the top card. Colour the diamond to look like an eyeball. Spread the colour over the edges of the diamond too.

Draw a sickly beast

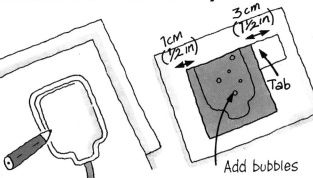

Draw a tube going from the beast to the bottle.

On the top card, draw a beast in a hospital bed. Draw a bottle for blood 2cm (¾in) from the top and 2cm(¾in) from the edge of the card. Cut out the bottle shape.

Fill the bottle with beastly blood

3cm (1½in)

1cm (½in)

Tab

Add bubbles

Lay the beast card over a piece of stiff white paper. Draw around inside the bottle shape. Lift off the card.

Add 1cm around the shape, and a 3cm(1½in) tab. Colour it green (but not the tab) and cut it out.

22

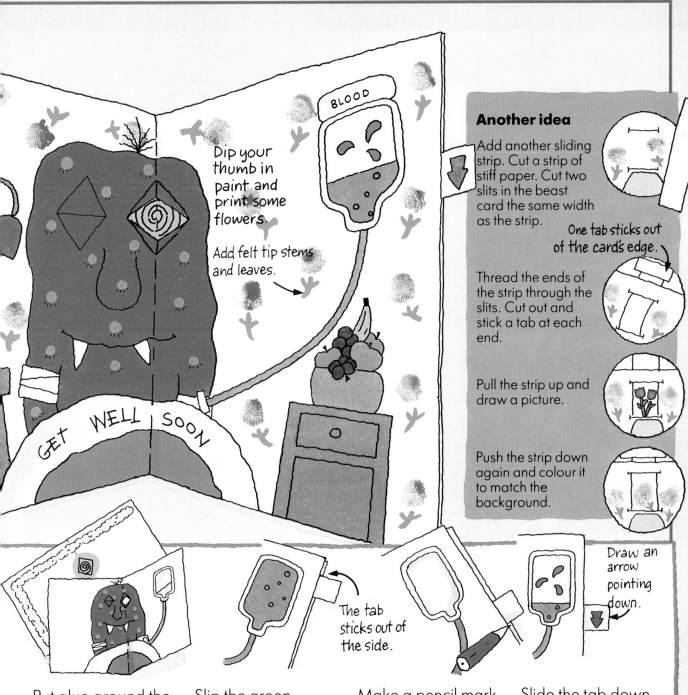

Dip your thumb in paint and print some flowers.

Add felt tip stems and leaves.

BLOOD

GET WELL SOON

Another idea

Add another sliding strip. Cut a strip of stiff paper. Cut two slits in the beast card the same width as the strip.

One tab sticks out of the card's edge.

Thread the ends of the strip through the slits. Cut out and stick a tab at each end.

Pull the strip up and draw a picture.

Push the strip down again and colour it to match the background.

The tab sticks out of the side.

Draw an arrow pointing down.

Put glue around the top, bottom and left-hand edge of the backing card. Stick the beast card on top.

Slip the green shape inside the card so the bottle is full. Slide it down gently until the bottle looks empty.

Make a pencil mark below the tab and slide it up again. Glue up the side of the card, as far as the mark.

Slide the tab down and draw splashes on the card behind. Slide the tab up and down to fill and empty the bottle.

23

Toothy bear

Make some snapping jaws

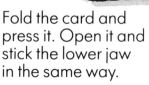

Fold a piece of brown or yellow card 21 x 28cm(8 x 11in).

Mark the fold, 6cm (2½in) from the top and 7cm(3in) from the bottom.

Take two smaller bits of the same coloured card and fold them.

Trace the bear's jaw templates on page 32 onto the cards. Cut them out.

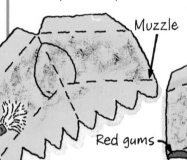

Muzzle

Black nose

Red gums

White teeth

Paint the bear's muzzle with a nearly dry brush and black paint.

Colour the rest of the jaw as shown. Colour the lower jaw the same way.

Put glue on the upper jaw tabs Fold them behind as mountain folds.

Place the point where the tabs meet onto the upper mark on the folded card.

Tip

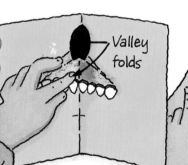

Valley folds

Match the middle of the tabs to the lower mark.

Valley fold

You may find it easier to press one tab into place, then the other.

Press the centre folds in the jaw and nose into valley folds.

Fold the card and press it. Open it and stick the lower jaw in the same way.

Pull out the jaw. Press the centre fold in the lower jaw to make a valley fold.

24

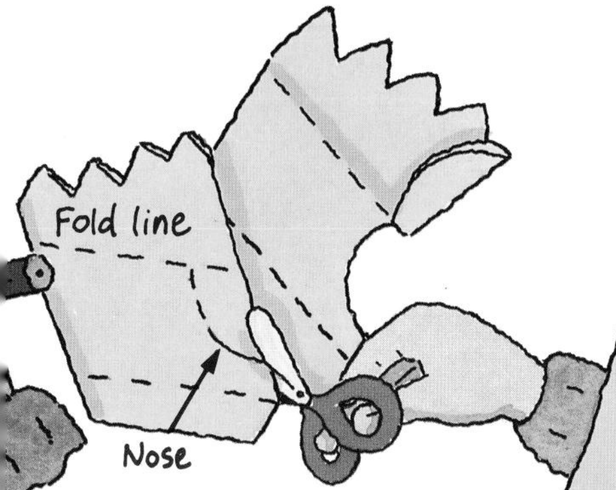

Fold line

Nose

Cut around the nose to the fold line. Crease all the fold lines both ways.

Tabs' edges meet here

Stick the tabs down. Make sure that their short edges meet along the centre fold.

Close the card and press it. Open it again to make the jaws snap.

To finish the bear

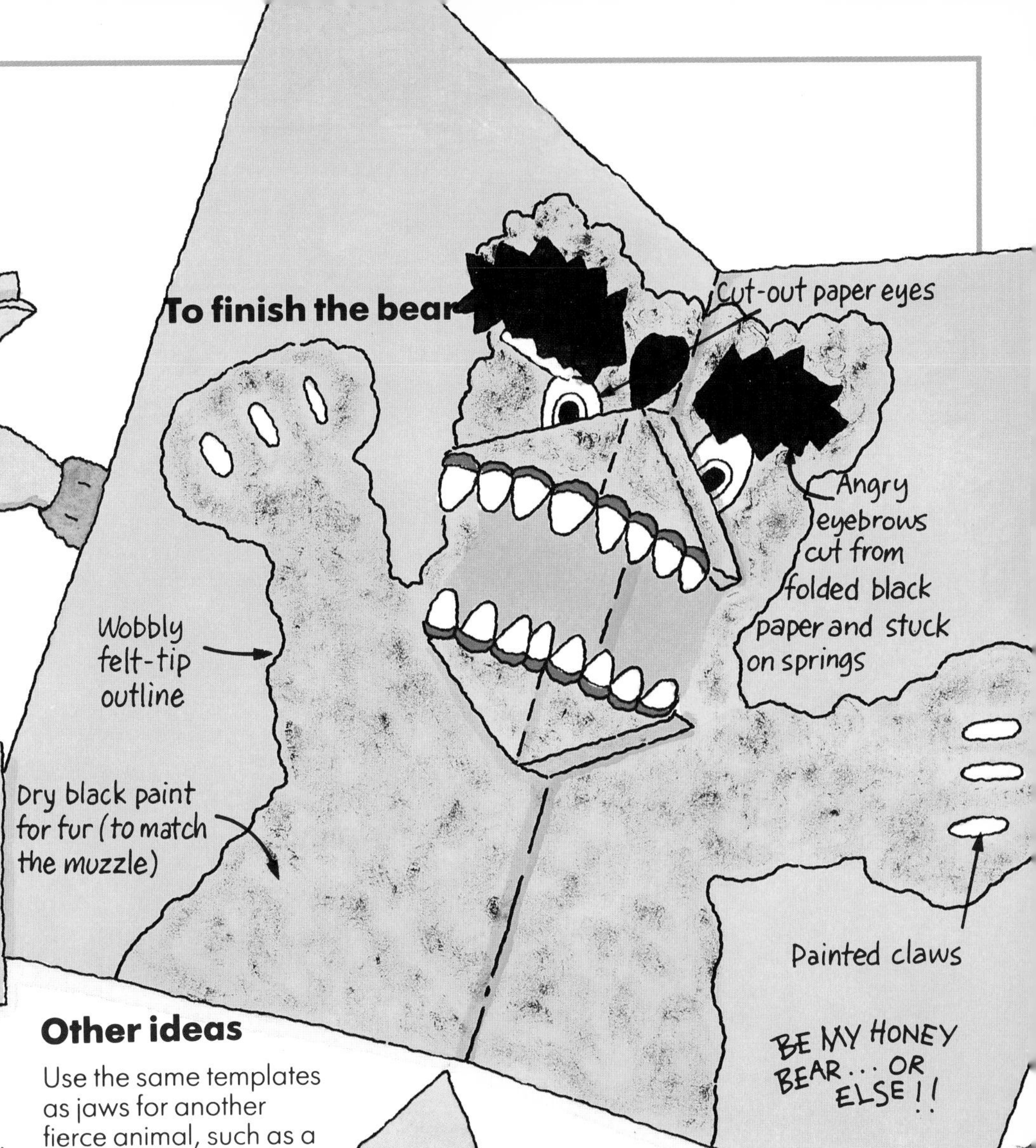

Cut-out paper eyes

Wobbly felt-tip outline

Dry black paint for fur (to match the muzzle)

Angry eyebrows cut from folded black paper and stuck on springs

Painted claws

BE MY HONEY BEAR... OR ELSE!!

Other ideas

Use the same templates as jaws for another fierce animal, such as a shark.

Shark

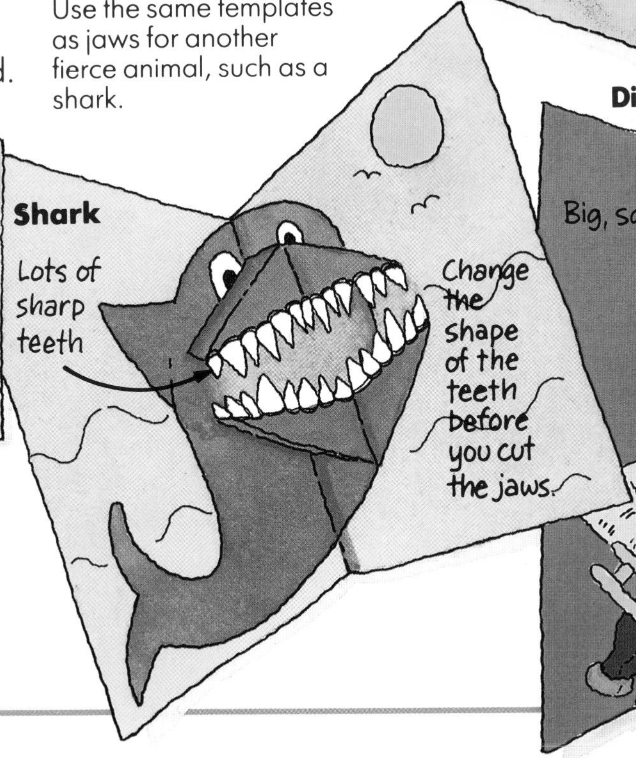

Lots of sharp teeth

Change the shape of the teeth before you cut the jaws.

Digger

Big, square teeth

25

House of doom

This scary scene uses lots of pop-ups. On the next four pages you can find out how to make some of them. You can see how to make the rest by looking back to the page numbers given. You do not have to make all these pop-ups. You could add some of your own instead.

Spook

Twisted branches

Tumble-down walls

The background

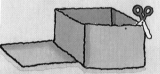

Cut the top and one side off a large box. Choose one made of thin card, so it is easy to cut.

Line the box with coloured paper. Paint a spooky black background and floor.

Trim off the edges and corners to make jagged turret and tree shapes.

Rat in a cage

Make a card with a box fold in it (see page 18). Cut thin strips to the fold line. Open the card.

Pull up every other strip to make the bars of the cage. Glue one side to the floor of the box.

Stick a paper rat inside. Close the card and stick extra paper on the top to hide the rat.

Clock striking midnight

Bat and moon

Stick a moon on the background. Make a bat and glue its wing-tips so it overlaps the moon.

Flapping owl (page 4)

Stick a cut-out owl on a flap-up card. Add fierce-looking eyes .

Mummy (page 20)

Cut a door out of paper and glue a mummy inside. Paint around and behind the mummy with black paint.

Colourful spook (page 14)

Make a card with a box fold. Cut one end into a curved door shape. Make an inkblot spook and stick it onto the box.

To close the pop-ups

Glue the pop-ups inside the box. Make sure you stick them so they open out the right way.

Using a ball point pen, make a small hole near the open edge of each pop-up.

Poke paper fasteners through from behind each hole. Open them out to hold the doors shut.

Tree with blinking eyes

Snip the top of the paper into branch shapes.

Paint a tree trunk inside the box. Stick some red paper onto it. Cut a piece of black paper big enough to cover it.

Cut eyeholes near the bottom of the black paper. Put glue along the sides and bottom. Stick it over the red paper.

Leave the top edge unglued. A pair of red eyes should show through the eyeholes. Draw in the eyeballs.

Slide a long piece of black paper into the paper "pocket". Move it up and down to make the eyes open and close.

27

Beckoning hand

On a piece of folded paper draw a nightgown sleeve. with a tab at the end. Draw in a fold line as shown. Cut the sleeve out.

Bend the sleeve both ways along the fold line. Cut a door from folded black card. Put glue on the tab. Stick the sleeve near the bottom of the door.

Bend the sleeve along the fold line, so it lifts when you open the door. Colour the tab black. Stick the door inside the box.

Cut out and stick a ghostly hand inside the sleeve edge nearest to you. When you open and close the door, the hand will beckon.

Snake

Draw a spiral shape. Start in the middle and work outwards. Draw snake patterns, eyes and nostrils.

Cut around the edge. Then cut in towards the middle, following the line of the spiral.

Make a trap door

Draw a circle on folded paper and cut it out. Leave an uncut "hinge" at the folded edge.

Glue each end of the snake to one half of the trap door. Stick the trap to the floor of the box.

Skeleton

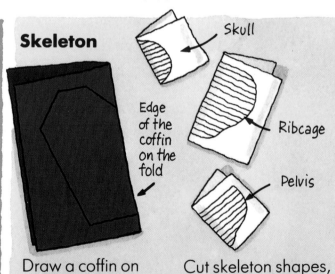

Draw a coffin on folded black paper and cut it out.

Cut skeleton shapes, using the mummy technique (page 20).

High-rise ghost

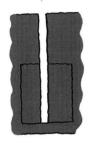

Slit

Cut the top off a small box. Paint it black. Cut a slit at the back, from the top almost to the bottom.

Hold the box in position inside the large box and draw around it. Cut a matching slit in the large box, as shown.

Put sticky tape at the top to seal the slit. Glue the small box in place so that the slits line up.

To make the ghost

Add arms on springs

Accordion fold a strip of paper. Stick a cut-out ghost on the top (see page 5).

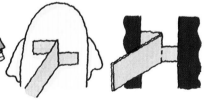

Cut a strip of stiff card. Cut a slit at one end. Bend the ends opposite ways.

Other ideas

Instead of a box you could make a pop-up book.

Make several pop-up cards of the same size. Stick them back-to-back to make a book.

Write a ghost story for your book. You could use gold or silver pen to write out the words.

Try out different ideas for stories with other sorts of pop-ups.

Glue the ends to the back of the ghost. Thread the card strip through the slit in the box.

Stick the end of the folded paper strip to the floor of the turret.

Slide the card strip up to make the ghost pop up.

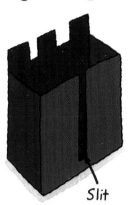

Black paint around skeleton

Paint arm and leg bones

Glue the skeleton inside the coffin, matching the folds.

Spinning wheel

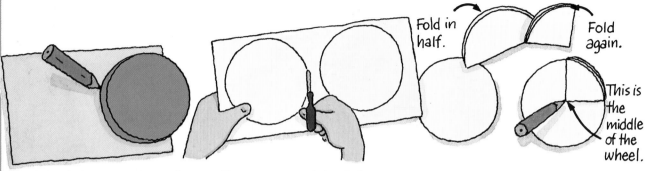

Put a jar lid on a piece of card so that it overlaps the edge. Draw around it.

Draw around the lid twice more on paper and cut out two wheel shapes.

Fold one wheel in four. Lay it over the other wheel and make a mark by the point.

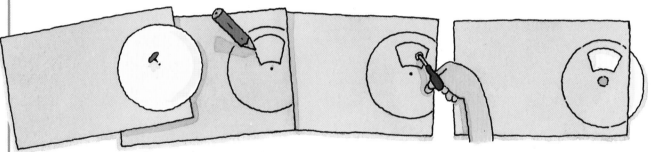

Put the open wheel over the circle on the card. Push a pin through the middle to make a hole in the circle.

Inside the circle draw a window above the pinhole and cut it out.

Put the wheel under the card and push a paper fastener through both pinholes.

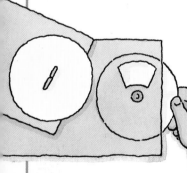
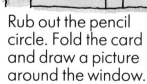

Open out the fastener. Spin the wheel to make sure it moves freely.

Rub out the pencil circle. Fold the card and draw a picture around the window.

Draw more pictures through the window onto the wheel, turning as you go.

You could add a spinning wheel to a pop-up card.

Templates

To make some of the cards in this book, you need to trace the templates (outline shapes) on this page and the next.

How to trace a template

Keep the paper in place with paperclips.

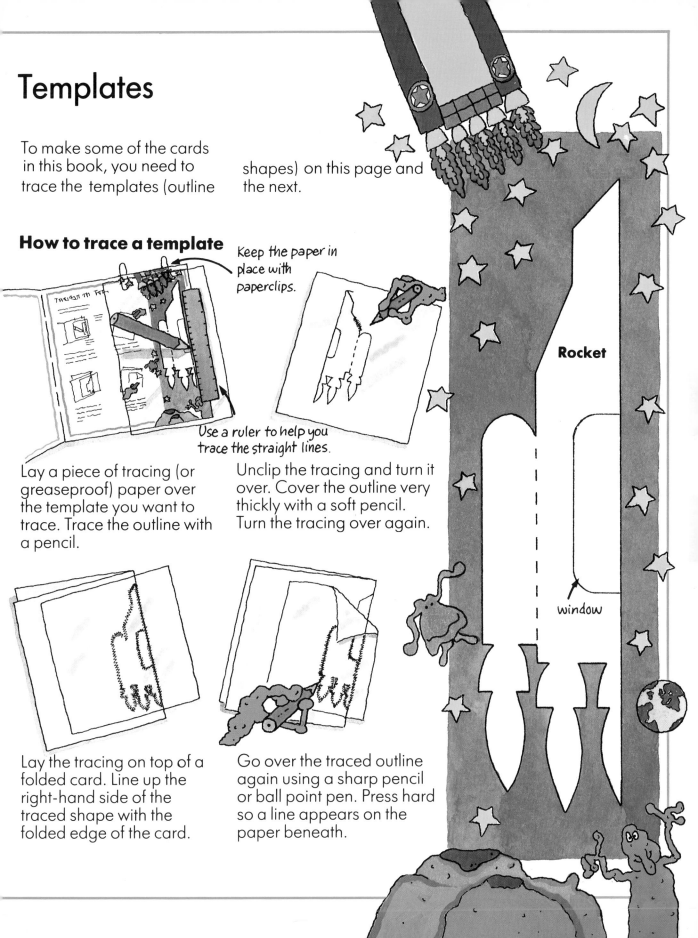

Use a ruler to help you trace the straight lines.

Lay a piece of tracing (or greaseproof) paper over the template you want to trace. Trace the outline with a pencil.

Unclip the tracing and turn it over. Cover the outline very thickly with a soft pencil. Turn the tracing over again.

Lay the tracing on top of a folded card. Line up the right-hand side of the traced shape with the folded edge of the card.

Go over the traced outline again using a sharp pencil or ball point pen. Press hard so a line appears on the paper beneath.

Rocket

window

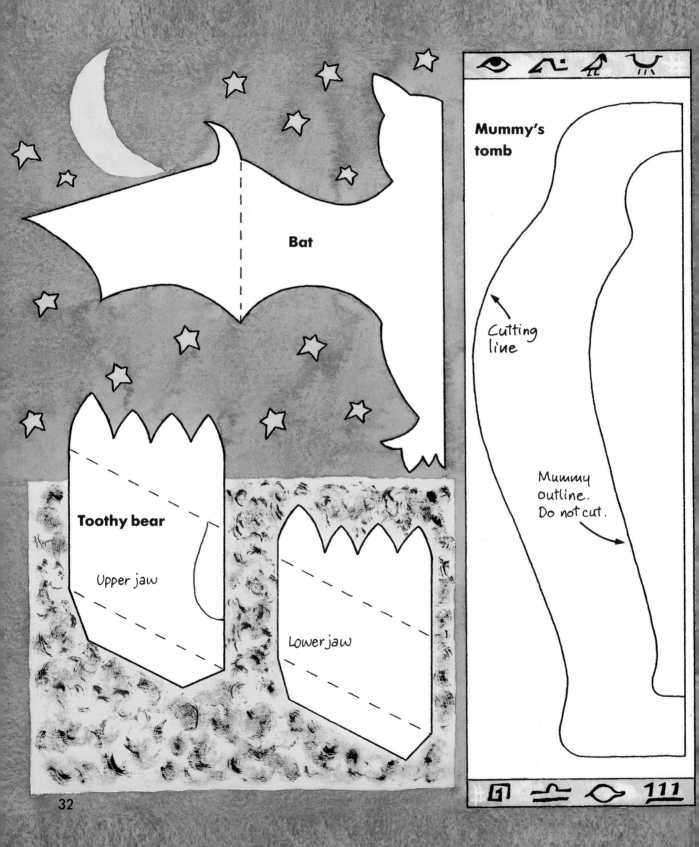

Bat

Mummy's tomb

Cutting line

Mummy outline. Do not cut.

Toothy bear

Upper jaw

Lower jaw

111